♥

This igloo book belongs to:

....

igloobooks

This edition published in 2013
by Igloo Books Ltd
Cottage Farm
Sywell
NN6 0BJ
www.igloobooks.com

Text and illustrations © 2009 Humphrey's Corner Limited

www.humphreys-corner.com

Adapted from Humphrey's Bedtime
First published in 2000 by The Penguin Group

FIR003 0913
4 6 8 10 9 7 5 3
ISBN: 978-1-78197-300-4

Printed and manufactured in China

Humphrey's Bedtime

Sally Hunter

It was Baby Jack's bedtime.

Humphrey and Lottie tucked him in.
"Night, night, sleep tight," they said.

Baby Jack had to go first because he was the smallest.
Next, it was Humphrey's bedtime.

Lottie said, "I am allowed to stay up very, very late.
That's because I'm the biggest."

Humphrey got his toys ready for bath time.

He made big bubble mountains...

... and magic potions.

Humphrey had a lovely time.

Lottie wasn't getting ready for bed.
She said her babies needed a really good wash!

"PJs on, Humphrey," mum said.

Humphrey had hot milk and buttery toast.

He felt warm and cozy in his tummy.

Mop liked his, too.

But Lottie didn't have time for supper.
She said, "oh, no... it's my babies' tea time.
Eat it all up and you will grow big and strong."

Humphrey had a horsey ride!

"Neigh! Neigh! Up the wooden hill to bed."

Humphrey had fun seeing how high he could fly.
Mum said, "I think it's story time now!"

It was Humphrey's special book.

"Once upon a time, a little pixie lived
at the bottom of the garden," said Mum.

Humphrey was all snuggly ... and sleepy.

Humphrey didn't hear how the pixie and his friends lived happily ever after because he fell asleep before the end.

ssssh... goodnight, little Humphrey. x

Lottie still wasn't getting ready for bed!
She was having problems with her babies.

Lulu was being silly.

Trevor wouldn't get ready for bed properly.

Barry wouldn't lie down...

... and Bear had got lost.

Lottie felt all hot...

... and CROSS!

Daddy came in from work. "What's all this?"
he asked. "Come on, my funny little girl."

"Off we go," he said.

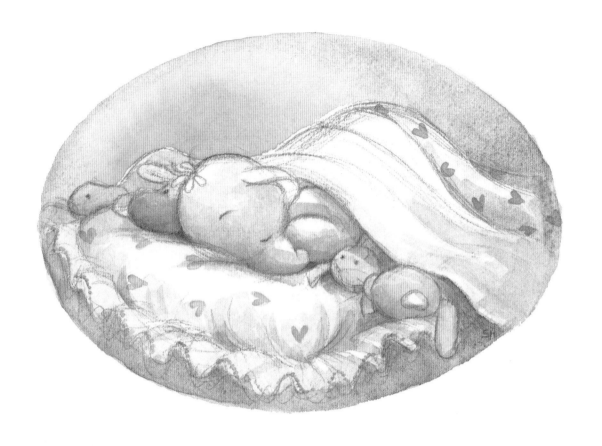

"To bed."

Goodnight,
Baby Jack, Humphrey and Lottie.
Sweet Dreams. x